Robbie's World

And His SPECTRUM of Adventures!

Book 1

Chapters 1-4

Story and Illustrations by
Cindy Gelormini (Robbie's Mama)

Xulon Press

Xulon Press
2301 Lucien Way #415
Maitland, FL 32751
407.339.4217
www.xulonpress.com

Printed in the United States of America.

Paperback ISBN-13: 978-1-6322-1846-9

Hardcover ISBN-13: 978-1-6322-1847-6

Ebook ISBN-13: 978-1-6322-1848-3

Dedicated to: All my Bubbas

Robbie is a penguin who likes riding in the car.

His Mama always says, "I love you just the way you are."

Chapter 1

Daycare and the Doctor

When Robbie was a baby he learned things a little slow.
His Mama always thought,
"Oh, he'll catch up one day I know."

Mama liked to hold him when he didn't want to walk.

Robbie was so sweet and quiet. He rarely ever talked.

When Robbie went to daycare, other penguins liked to play.

But Robbie liked the puddles.

He could splash and SPLASH all day!

7

Every morning all the penguins sat for circle time.

But Robbie didn't like to sit, he got up every time!

8

At snack time, many times, his water bottle made him choke.

The other penguins laughed, they thought it was a silly joke!

He was the only little penguin who refused to eat his fishies.

He didn't like the taste of anything all wet and squishy!

Some penguins liked to play with trucks and push the cars ahead.

But Robbie like to line up all the cars and trucks instead!

10

When Teacher said,
"It's clean up time!
Toys go in the bin!"

Robbie liked to run instead

and spin and spin

and **spin!**

Teacher talked to Mama and said,
"Robbie doesn't talk.
He likes to flap his flippers and
he really likes to rock!

He doesn't pay attention and
he doesn't play with blocks.

I know a **Special** Teacher
who will love him lots and lots!"

Mama picked up Robbie and she kissed him seven times.
Mama looked at teacher and said,
"Thank you." and "Goodbye".

She fastened Robbie's seatbelt
as she put him in the car.
She looked at him and said,

*"I love you just
the way you are."*

15

Mama called the Doctor and he said to come on in.

Robbie got up on the table and let Doctor look at him.

"Mama are you giving Robbie all his vitamins?"

"Robbie, open up, say 'Ah'" but Robbie only grinned.

Hmmmm," the Doctor said, because it seemed he couldn't hear.

"Does he speak?" the Doctor asked, and looked in Robbie's ears.

Robbie didn't like that, so he screamed out loud in fear!

But Mama sang his favorite tune and wiped away his tears.

17

Doctor asked more questions, "Does he choke? Does he spin?

Does he never look at you or answer when you call to him?

Does he like to run away and does he never sit still?"

Mama said, "How did you know? Will you give him a pill?"

Doctor said, "It's Autism." and wrote it in his chart.

He handed Mama books and said, "Here's a place to start".

"He may never speak." He said, "Prepare, this will be hard.

He won't say 'I want juice' or 'We go bye-bye in the car'.

He won't look you in the eyes and he may not know who you are.

He may never say 'I love you' and this news may break your heart."

Mama first stared into space because her mind was very far.

But she looked at little Robbie, he was still her little star.

Mama picked up Robbie and she kissed him seven times.

Mama looked at Doctor and said "Thank you." and "Goodbye".

She fastened Robbie's seatbelt
as she put him in the car.

She looked at him and said,

"I love you just the way you are."

Mama called up Papa when she started up the car.
"When you get done with work
just come and meet us at the park."

23

Then Mama
prayed to God to
help her find out
how to start
to be the
strongest Mama
to the boy who
stole her heart.

Mama sat and told him all the things the Doctor said,
while Robbie splashed in puddles and
the water splashed his head.

"He may never be a baseball star, or be the President.
But God chose us to love a very special boy instead."

25

Papa picked up little Robbie and he put him in the car.
He kissed him seven times and said,
"You're still my little star".

Papa looked at Mama and he took her in his arms.
Then they said to little Robbie,

"We love you just the way you are."

27

Mom's Minute

When Robbie was a toddler he said a few words, but by the time he was two and a half, he stopped talking. Signs of Autism are usually first noticed around the age of two because of the absence of speech, and other behaviors begin to emerge. Autism is not diagnosed like other disorders or syndromes. There is no blood test that can be taken. The way it's diagnosed is by asking questions and observing a child's behaviors, similar to how the Doctor does in our story. Usually the first ones to notice the signs of Autism are a Daycare or Pre-School Teacher. Many parents are usually in denial of their child's symptoms and don't take the information very well. That's why Robbie's Mama in this story says "Thank you and Goodbye!"

A Developmental Pediatrician was the first to give Robbie a formal diagnosis of Autism. From what I knew of Autism, the children were in their own world and were not affectionate. But that description did not fit Robbie, so I didn't believe the Doctor. It was not until I read the booklet that the Doctor gave me, where another Mama described her son, that I finally realized that maybe the Doctor was right. I have a feeling when other parents read this book series, they may feel the same way.

When Robbie's Dad and I heard the news and finally accepted it, it was very difficult. Up until then we thought we had a "normal" child, and like most parents, had hopes and dreams for his future. Then suddenly, it seemed like we were told that our child was not the child we thought he was. Instead, we now had a child with a disability. It was as though the Robbie we thought we knew was gone, and now we had a different child. We had to go through a mourning process, and then come to love and accept this new child. One day as I was praying about it, I felt God say to me "Just love him the way he is." ...so simple, yet so profound, and yet it guided me throughout Robbie's life. I loved every little quirky thing he did and gave him all the love, hugs and kisses that he would tolerate. I also learned to become his fierce protector and advocate. In return, he taught me how to become strong, patient, forgiving and then the greatest lesson of all, how to love unconditionally. This lesson is now the main theme of the book series where you'll hear repeatedly, "I love you just the way you are."

Autism Behaviors

When Robbie was diagnosed I was given a chart similar to this. I was told if a child has eight or more of these symptoms or behaviors, he has Autism. If he has less than eight of these, it's considered PDD-NOS "Pervasive Developmental Disorder-Not Otherwise Specified". At the time, he exhibited about five of the behaviors and was diagnosed with PDD-NOS. As he grew older however, he developed almost all of the symptoms/behaviors in this chart. He never learned to speak and was eventually diagnosed with Severe Autism.

Inappropriate laughing or giggling.

Difficulty in interacting with others.

No real fear of dangers.

May not want cuddling.

Inappropriate response or no response to sound.

May avoid eye contact.

May prefer to be alone.

Apparent insensitivity to pain.

Insistence on sameness.

Inappropriate attachments to objects.

Echoes words or phrases.

Spins objects or self.

Sustained unusual or repetitive play,

Difficulty in expressing needs. May use gestures.

Chapter 2

Waddle Scouts
and Ice Cream

Robbie's older sisters liked to go to Waddle Scouts.
Robbie came along while Robbie's Mama
helped them out.

Robbie didn't like to sit. He ran and ran around.
Even when his Mama said,
"Now Robbie, you sit down!"

While all the little penguin girls were singing songs aloud,

Mama looked and saw that he was nowhere to be found!

They searched the whole room over. They were looking all about, when they saw the door was opened. Robbie must have run right out!

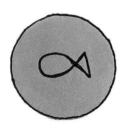  

Mama ran outside and asked,
"Tell me, did you see
a little penguin boy run by, and he is only three?"

"Oh yes." The other penguins said,
"We saw him running free.

He ran over toward the river
running underneath the trees."

Mama ran and found him and said,
"Never run that far!

What if I couldn't find you or
I did not know where you are?"

But Robbie didn't understand
that he had run too far,

or what his Mama said,
or what dangers really are.

Mama picked up Robbie and
she kissed him seven times.

She brought him back inside and said,
"It's time to say goodbye."

Mama felt relieved and buckled Robbie in the car.

She said, "I'm GLAD to have you back.

I love you just the way you are."

Mama buckled up and started
driving down the street.
Robbie watched where she was going,
leaning over in his seat.

Then as they turned the corner
Robbie kicked and kicked the seat,
flapped his flippers on his head,
and began to scream and scream.

Mama figured out why he was
causing such a scene.

They had headed toward the pool
but then kept driving down the street.

"It's no longer Summer time,
the pool is closed right now you see."

"I know!" Mama changed the subject.

"Who wants some
ice cream?!"

Mama turned the car and headed toward the ice cream shop.

She put on Papa's music. (He likes Oldies and Doo Wop.)

Robbie stopped his fussing. Music always makes him stop.

Then finally he smiled, as they pulled in the parking lot.

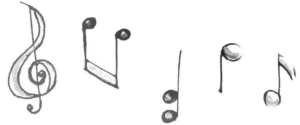

46

When they went in they saw

a whole long line inside the door...

49

But Robbie hates to wait
and threw himself down on the floor!

Everybody looked at his commotion in the store.

His sisters rolled their eyes and said,
"Here we go once more!"

A Grandma turned and said,
"You should be a better Mama.
Clearly he is spoiled,
we can tell from all this drama."

Mama took a great big breath
and thought of what to say.
"His meltdown is from Autism.
Bless your heart,
have a nice day."

Mama ordered ice cream cones and
one was dipped in fudge.

Another Mama whispered,
"It was not her place to judge."

Robbie ate his ice cream and his sisters ate theirs too.
Then the cashier said,
"Somebody else already paid for you."

Mama looked around and she almost began to cry.

She carried Robbie to the car and kissed him seven times.

57

As she put him in his seat she said,
"Today's been rough so far.

But always, always know,

*I love you
just the way you are.*"

Mom's Minute

In Chapter 2 we meet Robbie's twin sisters! They love Robbie dearly and were like two more little Mommies. was their Brownie leader and Robbie really did run away during a Brownie meeting just like in the story. The girls went to Salt Brook School where there was a brook in the woods behind the school. Robbie was actually only around two years old and was wearing a diaper and still drinking a bottle when he ran away, yet the parents in the parking lot never bothered to realize that he was running away without a parent present!

Running away like this is called "**eloping**" and is common among children with Autism. They also **LOVE the water**! So usually if they elope they are headed toward a body of water somewhere, whether it's a pool, brook, river or the ocean. Drowning is a real concern, so this is why it's very important for them to learn how to swim at an early age. Robbie attended a school for children with Autism and they took regular school trips to the YWCA for swimming lessons where he learned how to swim. Eventually they built a new, larger school, with two swimming pools, where students learned how to swim daily. Robbie learned to be a good swimmer!

Robbie also loved music, as most people with Autism do. Taking a ride in the car and playing music always calmed him down. After summer was over, Robbie really did kick and scream like in this story because he wanted to go to the pool. Robbie also loved ice cream, (who doesn't?) but hated waiting in lines and going to stores. So eventually I just stopped taking him out in public! This is another skill his school worked on with their students. They took the kids on trips to teach them how to wait in line and go to stores without having meltdowns. As in this story, many who are not familiar with Autism may misinterpret these meltdowns as "spoiled children". But usually the cause is a **sensory overload**, or, in Robbie's case, he just didn't understand the world around him and why he had to be there, or why he had to wait.

People like Robbie that can't speak, also don't understand why things happen in the world. If you try to explain things to them, they don't understand. So a little dose of kindness, compassion and understanding will go a long way.

Chapter 3

Fireworks and Firemen

Robbie liked the Summer time. He liked to be outside,
jumping on the trampoline and going for car rides,
and playing on the playground when he went to
Summer School. But his favorite thing of all
was swimming in Aunt Rosie's pool!

On weekends Robbie's family went
to visit and to swim.

Robbie had no fear of water, so he'd just jump right in!

Mama put his floaties on before he'd go get in.

"Put these on," she said, "my silly little penguin!"

Aunt Rosie loved to cook.
Her homemade meatballs were the best!
Robbie loved to eat them. You'd have two, he'd eat the rest!

He didn't like her flowers though, he didn't like the smell.

The fragrance was so strong it hurt his nose, so he would yell!

He liked the summertime parade and firetrucks as well, but
held his flippers on his ears because he didn't like the bell.

His sisters marched in the parade with all the Waddle Scouts.

But mostly Robbie loved that they threw candy all about!

69

The family had a barbeque on Independence Day.
His sisters and his cousins ran together off to play.

But Robbie was content alone, to swim and splash all day.

His Mama kept her eyes on him, in case he ran away.

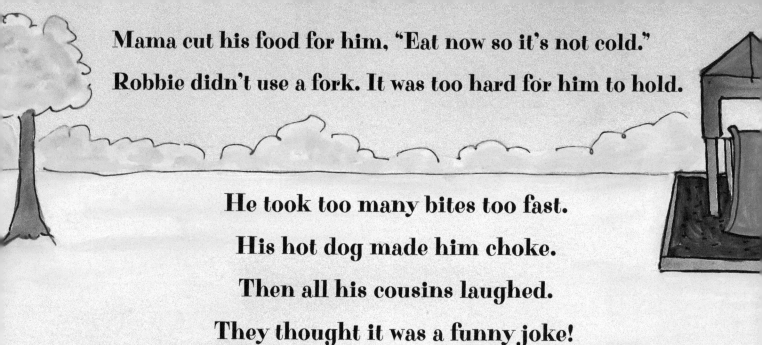

Mama cut his food for him, "Eat now so it's not cold."

Robbie didn't use a fork. It was too hard for him to hold.

He took too many bites too fast.

His hot dog made him choke.

Then all his cousins laughed.

They thought it was a funny joke!

Mama said, "Are you OK?" then kissed him seven times.

Then made sure Robbie slowed down and ate one bite at a time.

She helped him with his fork and said, "I know that this is hard.

But that's OK my son,

I love you just that way you are."

Papa yelled to everyone,
"It's starting to get dark!

It's time for
fireworks,
so let's all
head off to
the park!"

Everybody carried off their blankets and their chairs.
Mama worried booming fireworks
would make her Robbie scared.

Everybody in the town had gathered on the lawn.

Pop Pop sat down in his chair and he began to yawn.

Mama sat up Robbie's chair for him to sit upon.

Then she turned around and yelled out,

"Where is Robbie? He is gone!"

Everybody jumped up and began to look around.

How would they ever find him in the midst of this big crowd?

Mama ran out toward the street and Papa toward the lake.

"We never should have come tonight, this was a big mistake!"

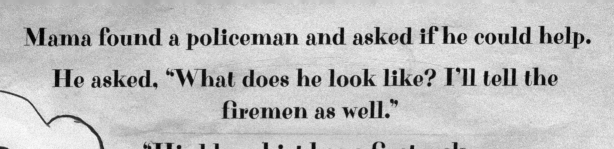

Mama found a policeman and asked if he could help.

He asked, "What does he look like? I'll tell the firemen as well."

"His blue shirt has a firetruck with a little yellow bell.

But he acts like he can't hear you and won't answer if you yell".

79

The Policeman called the firemen and the rescue workers too.

He told them all to "Be advised, that he won't answer you."

They looked and looked for Robbie as the sky was growing dark.
Mama feared the worst and almost fainted in the park.

Then someone started waving, it was Papa in the distance.

He was shouting out, and Mama tried real hard to listen.

The fireworks began to boom and made it hard to hear.

She ran to Papa and heard him say,

"They found him!
Over here!"

A firefighter found him on
the fifty-yard line,
twirling around and laughing,
and having a good old time!

Mama was so angry she began to yell, then paused.
This silly boy had no idea the chaos that he caused.

She scooped him up and said,
"Robbie don't ever do that again!"
Then squeezed him tight and kissed him
seven times upon his head.

They watched the fireworks that night
locked safely in the car.
Mama shook her head and said,

*"I love you just the way
you are."*

Mom's Minute

Autism can affect a person's five senses of sight, sound, smell, taste, and touch. They can be either hyper or hypo sensitive. Although Robbie didn't have all of these hyper sensitive issues, I added them to the story to reflect typical traits of Autism.

1. **Sight** – Robbie's sight seemed to be fine, but he did things to stimulate his sight all the time. He would constantly squint, closing one eye, and then shake or flap things in front of his eyes as stimulation. This is called "Stimming". In most of the Photos of Robbie when he was young he is always closing one eye.

2. **Sound** – Many kids with Autism are very sensitive to sounds like firetruck horns and noisy places and may cover their ears and get very upset in spaces that are too crowded and noisy.

3. **Smell** – Sometimes their sense of smell may be hyper sensitive. I remember another Mom telling a story of her son that screamed every time they drove past a house that had a lot of roses because he couldn't tolerate the smell.

4. **Taste** – Robbie, like most Autistic kids, was a very picky eater. He never ate anything wet or squishy, like pasta, fruit or vegetables, with the exception of sweet stuff like ice cream, chocolate pudding and cereal with milk. When he was a toddler he did choke on his food almost every time he ate. But I think it was more of a tactile issue than a taste issue, because it seemed more that he couldn't tolerate the textures in his mouth. He did love meatballs, but with NO TOMATO SAUCE! We always thought he wouldn't eat pizza either until one day the pizza box was missing and we found that he had taken it into his room and ate about 6 slices in his room!

5. **Touch** – Many Autistic kids have "tactile defensiveness" which means their sense of touch is hyper sensitive and their nerves can feel on edge. They may not like the feeling of being touched, or shoes on their feet, or scratchy clothes. Therapists will use techniques like applying pressure

to the joints, or brushing the limbs to calm the nerves. Wearing weighted vests can keep their nerves calm and using weighted blankets can help them sleep better. The reason Robbie loved the water is because it calmed his nerves, and so did the pressure of jumping on the trampoline.

Robbie's Dad was a fireman and marched in the parade each year. We did also go to Aunt Rosie's house to swim. As for the story of him running away at the fireworks, oh yes! That really happened exactly the way it does in this story! He almost gave me a heart attack! After that, we didn't go to the fireworks until about 15 years later!

Robbie and the girls meeting Dad at the fire-house after Robbie's first parade!

Robbie's sisters marching with their school in the parade.

Robbie had no fear of the water! He would jump in and open his eyes under the water and laugh!

Robbie loved jumping on the trampoline, but loved it even more when his sisters jumped with him! This was a time when they could actually get some good eye contact from him.

Chapter 4

Special Learning School

When Robbie was a toddler
he had specialists for speech.

They thought he couldn't hear
because they never heard him speak.

But then as he got older
they could tell that he could hear.
His specialist told Mama, "This is Autism I fear."

She said she'd help his Mama find a school that's right for him.

They'd know just how to handle when he screams and when he stims.

94

"We'll visit different schools and find a good one I am sure."

But at every one they'd visit, Robbie ran right for the door!

The Special Learning School was the last tour of the day.

Mama watched in case her Robbie tried to run away.

Instead he found a toy he liked and sat down with it to play.

Mama laughed, "I think he has decided that we'll stay!"

So Robbie started his new school right on his third birthday.

Mama was so worried. She stayed home and cried and prayed.

She had no way of knowing what was happening all day.

All she could do was watch the clock and pace the floor and wait.

Finally at 3:00 she ran to meet the bus.

Was Robbie happy and content? Did he scream and make a fuss?

She can't ask him how his day went. He won't answer, he can't speak.

But when she saw him he was smiling, and had kisses on his cheeks!

98

Mama took his backpack, opened up to take a look.

She took out Robbie's lunchbox and inside she found a book.

His teacher wrote inside it, and her name was Mrs. Snow.

"Robbie's day was great! I'll write each day to let you know."

So, Mama got him dressed each day in time to catch the bus.

Sometimes he wasn't in the mood and he'd begin to fuss.

Mama had to calm him, holding tight to make him hush.

Then that would make them late, then Mama had to make him rush.

He didn't like his school clothes, or the way they made him feel.

Sometimes he'd flap his flippers on his head and then he'd squeal.

He didn't like his buttons or his snow boots on his feet,
and forget a hat upon his head, he'd throw it in the street!

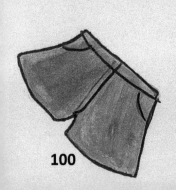

Robbie put his coat on when he stopped pitching a fit.
Then he ran out to the bus and he leaned in to get a kiss.
Miss Nina drove his bus and they had started a routine.

"Good morning Robbie!"
she would say,

then she would
kiss his cheek.

One of Robbie's classmates was obsessed with counting cars.
He'd say "Hello Robbie's Mama, who rides in the big green car."
She'd give him a high five and say, "Good morning Anashwar!"
then buckle Robbie up and say, *"I love you just the way you are."*

Robbie liked his school and he had many specialists.
He really liked his teachers, but there was one he liked the best.

His aide was very funny
and his name was Mr. Glen.

He always made him smile and laugh.

He was Robbie's friend.

He worked with Robbie getting dressed,
and taught him some self-care,
like washing hands and brushing teeth
and even brushed his hair.

He taught him how to use a fork
and worked on how to wait.

When Robbie learned
to do new things,
they gave him lots of praise!

Robbie was so cute he was a hit with all the chicks!

The first day he was there one said, "Hey he's cute! Who's this?!"

Every day in circle time the girls would try to sit
on either side of Robbie, but he couldn't care one bit!

Everybody listened to what Mrs. Snow would say.

She told them all the plans for what they all would do that day.

The Art Teacher was coming and
they all liked that a bunch.

Then they would also go to gym
before they went to lunch.

Everybody lined up at the door
to stand and wait.

Robbie's waiting skills
were getting better every day.

But as they passed the lunch room on
the way to get to gym,

Robbie got upset. He thought
that they were going in.

108

Teacher tried to calm him down while
he was on the floor.
The more she tried to talk to him,
he just screamed more and more.

Then Mr. Glen came over,
got down on the floor with him,
got nose to nose with Robbie
until he began to grin.

Finally everybody got to go to their gym class.

Then came Art, and then came Speech Therapy after that.

Robbie had a picture book to ask for what he needs.

He handed Teacher pictures as a way for him to speak.

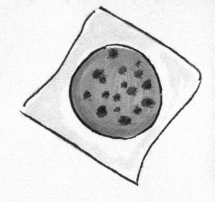

They taught him "yes" and "no"
and also taught him how to sign.

Every time he got it right,
they gave him a high five.

Speech class made him hungry.
It was time for lunch at last!

He did his best to stay in line,
and not to walk too fast!

Robbie carried his own tray and pushed it down the line.

"Do you want tater tots?" she asked, "Robbie, use your signs."

"Do you want peas?" she asked.

He shook his head from side to side!

His teachers used up every minute as a learning time.

Carefully he carried all his food to his class table.

He didn't even drop his milk, everything stayed stable.

He even used his fork and he was proud that he was able.

But the best thing that he learned was to stay

sitting at the table!

Soon the day was over.
They began to call each bus.

"Time to get our coats on, and our backpacks,
and line up!"

They listened 'til they heard them say,
"And now bus number ten!"

Robbie headed out the door and walked with Mr. Glen.

Miss Nina drove him home.

The ride was not so very far.

Miss Nina kissed his cheek and said,

"I'll see you Rob, tomorrow."

Mama stood outside
and waited by her big green car.

She took his hand
and walked in saying,

116

"I love you just the way you are."

Mom's Minute

When Robbie was 2 1/2 he stopped talking. I talked to another Mom who was a Speech Therapist and told her I hadn't heard Robbie say any words for a couple months, and her eyebrows raised up. Her reaction told me something was up. She recommended having his speech and hearing evaluated. I took him to the hospital for some tests and they determined that he was speech and hearing delayed. Since Robbie had several ear infections we thought the problem was that he could not hear high pitched sounds, and that was delaying his speech. I put him into an Early Intervention Program for Hearing Impaired children.

But as we went through the therapy, Robbie had no interest, and just threw tantrums and tried to leave the room. His therapist recommended that we have him evaluated for Autism. Next we took him to a Developmental Pediatrician who diagnosed him with "PDD-NOS" (Discussed in Chapter 1) This Doctor recommended that we visit the Developmental Learning Center. I didn't know what this school was. I thought his speech was just a little delayed due to the ear infections, and after getting tubes in his ears he would catch up. I did not consider my son to be "handicapped" or have "Special Needs".

The next step was to call the Board of Education in my town to have him evaluated. They determined that he was "Preschool Handicapped" and eligible for services to attend a school for children with Special Needs. Huh? We were assigned a Learning Disabilities Teacher Consultant (LDTC) who began taking us to look at schools for handicapped children, with children in wheelchairs who were severely handicapped. I was a bit shocked. Robbie really did run for the door at all of these schools. But on the day that we went to visit the Developmental Learning Center that the Doctor had recommended Robbie seemed to feel quite at home. I took it as a sign that we had found the right school for him.

The day Robbie turned three he went off to school just like in this story. In his Early Intervention classes I was there and part of the therapy. But now, I had to send him off on a bus alone, in a diaper and still on a bottle, and he didn't speak. It was pretty scary. But he really did come home with kisses on his cheeks, and everyone loved Robbie. He and Miss Nina became best buddies, and as he got older Mr. Glen became his favorite aide. Robbie loved his school and attended until he was 21 years old. It was his home away from home.

This is Robbie with Mr. Glen on a class trip picking pumpkins on a farm, and then on Halloween dressed up as a mechanic. In school they worked on self-help skills and Mr. Glen used to brush Robbie's hair and put gel in it every day and make a big fuss over him, telling him how good he looked. I saw a real change in Robbie this year and he really looked forward to going to school. I could tell he wanted to get dressed and look good every day. Mr. Glen was very fun, funny and upbeat which made going to school fun! Having a great attitude is so important. Although Robbie couldn't speak, he could read your body language, attitude and the tone of your voice. It's like he had a sixth sense about people. I believe a lot of kids do.

Non-verbal kids don't really understand the world and how it works. Imagine not being able to speak or understand words, and then trying to figure out what you are asking them to do. His school taught using "Positive Reinforcement". This is HUGE! Robbie wanted to do things the right way and didn't like to make mistakes. If he felt he did something wrong he would get very upset. The WRONG way to be with him was to yell, get angry and disapprove. The RIGHT way to get good behavior and positive results was to keep a really upbeat, positive attitude. That and lots of smiles, laughter and high fives saying "Great job Robbie!"

Here is Robbie in his first class when he had just turned three.

Robbie with the Music Teacher

The girls in his class always fought over who would get to sit next to Robbie!

CPSIA information can be obtained
at www.ICGtesting.com
Printed in the USA
BVHW051403220421
605637BV00012B/1740

9 781632 218469